DELETE

To my dear friend, Magdalen Russell – J.D.

For Natalie and Jonny and the two bad cats, Andre and Leo – J.B.

Text copyright © Joyce Dunbar 2012
Illustrations copyright © Jill Barton 2012
The right of Joyce Dunbar to be identified as the author and of Jill Barton
to be identified as the illustrator of this work has been asserted by them in accordance
with the Copyright, Designs and Patents Act, 1988 (United Kingdom).

First published in Great Britain in 2012 and in the USA in 2013 by
Frances Lincoln Children's Books, 74-77 White Lion
Street, London N1 9PF
www.franceslincoln.com

A catalogue record for this book is available from the British Library.

ISBN 978-1-84780-369-6

Illustrated with pencil and watercolour

Set in Latina MT
Printed in Dongguan, Guangdong, China by Toppan Leefung in June 2013

3 5 7 9 8 6 4

Puss Jekyll
Cat Hyde

Joyce Dunbar

Illustrated by Jill Barton

F

FRANCES LINCOLN
CHILDREN'S BOOKS

This is **Puss Jekyll**

Pet of the house.

Hear her purr

As she grooms

Her fur,

Or curls

On my lap

For a nap.

Furry, purry puss.

So tame, I think

She is almost

One of

Us.

Now comes Cat Hyde

Scourge of the mouse.

Hear her howl

On her midnight

Prowl.

See her crouch

    Then pounce

All fang and claw,

See the poor little

House mouse

Dangling

  From her

    Jaw.

This is Puss Jekyll

Dozy, lazy

Snoozy puss.

So cosy.

Any warm spot

In the house

Will do.

The plump cushion

Or wicker chair

Or that sunny

Dappled

Patch

On the stair.

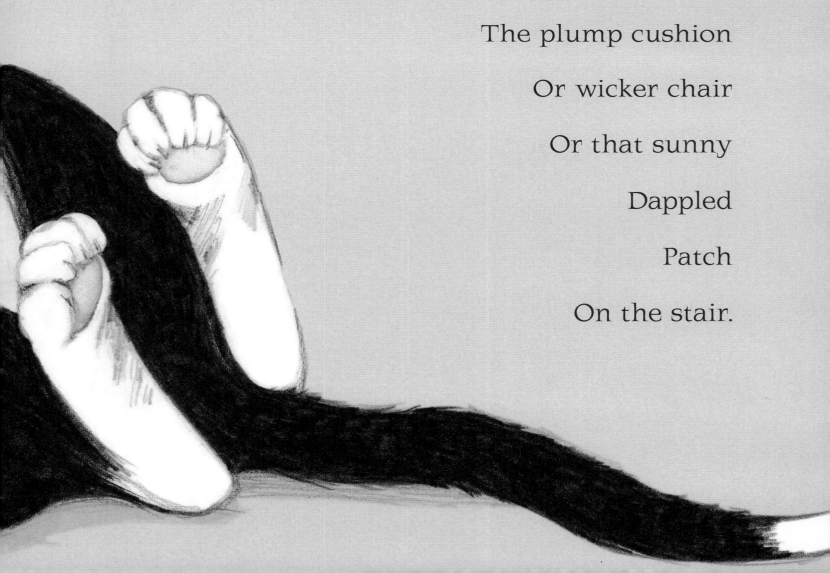

Now comes Cat Hyde

Ears pricked

Eyes wide.

Piercing

The dark

So stark

Scaring

      Daring.

Oh she can outglare

The barefaced moon

The owl

Or the fox

In his lair.

This is Puss Jekyll.

See the pink

Of a little tongue-tip

Lapping up

Sippy-sip, milk

From a bowl.

Then a wide

Wipe of nose

And whiskers

Face so clean

So saintly

Quaintly

Serene.

Now woe betide

Here comes Cat Hyde.

Pad pad

Through the mud

On the scent

On the track

Of blood

Fear and bone

Hunting the lone

Vole or shrew.

Anything tiny

And trembling

Will do.

This is Puss Jekyll

So charming

Disarming

Chasing

Skitter-scatter

That ball of wool

On the rug.

Then with a

Nonchalant

Innocent

Shrug

Folds in her claws

Tucks in her paws

So snug.

Now comes Cat Hyde

A warning in her

Sharp-toothed yawning.

Ravager

Savager

Devil cat, fiend

   Sly

Schemer and spoiler

Of dreams.

    Not for her the quick

    Clean kill

          But a long, lingering

          Merciless thrill.

This is Puss Jekyll

So refined,

With such grace,

She puts never a paw

Out of place.

How she soothes,

   Bewitches,

   Beguiles,

With her smooth,

Velvety wiles.

Sleek, sweet

Pussikins,

So meek and mild.

This is Cat Hyde

Night stalker

Roof walker

Fearless

Tearless

Street fighter

War torn

Love worn

Battered and

Tattered

Adored passionara

So wicked

And wild.

This is Puss Jekyll

Nuzzles up

Nose to nose.

How we love

To be close

Me and my pet!

And yet . . .

I have seen

More than dreams

In her glances and

Gleams. In her

Glares are the glints of

Nightmares!

Puss Jekyll, Cat Hyde

One cat, two names

    One wild, one tame.

Come the night

She changes faces

Casting off

Her daytime graces.

    Who is to blame

That my dear little

Kittikins

And this lynx-like

    Minx-like

    Sphynx-like

        Deceiver . . .

Are one
and the
same?